Gg Hh Ii Jj Kk Ll Mm

Uu Vv Ww Xx Yy Zz

Dear Parent,

The My First Steps to Reading® *series is based on a teaching activity that helps children learn to recognize letters and their sounds. The use of predictable language patterns and repetition of familiar words will also help your child build a basic sight vocabulary. Your child will enjoy watching the characters in the books place imaginative objects in "letter boxes." You and your child can even create and fill your own letter box, using stuffed animals, cut-out pictures, or other objects beginning with the same letter. The things you can do together are limited only by your imagination. Learning letters will be fun—the first important step on the road to reading.*

The Editors

My "m" Book

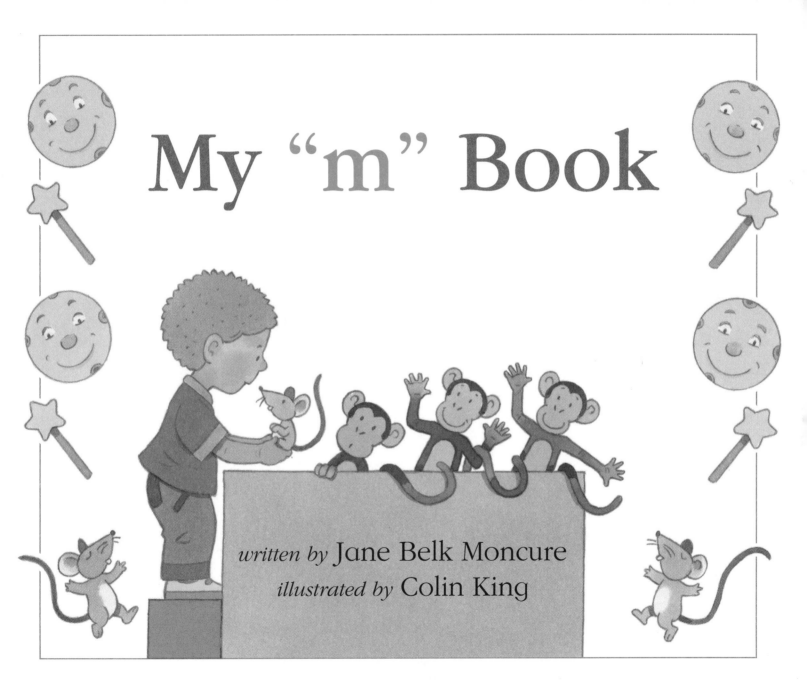

written by Jane Belk Moncure

illustrated by Colin King

Little  had a box.

"I will find things that begin
with my 'm' sound," he said.

"I will put them into my sound  box."

Little m found monkeys.

Did he put the monkeys into his box? He did.

Then Little  found a mouse.

Then he found another mouse

and another mouse.

He found many mice!

Did he put the mice into the box
with the monkeys? He did.

But the monkeys did not like the mice.

They jumped out of the box

and ran . . .

up a mountain.

Little **m** ran up the mountain.

The mice ran up the mountain, too.

Then the monkeys ran down the mountain.

The monkeys were so angry,
they did not see the

mud!

The monkeys fell into the mud!

What a mess!

Little  and the mice pulled the monkeys out of the mud.

Little  m put the monkeys
back into the box.

"Mice, be nice!" he said.

"I must find something else for my mice."

Just then,

Little  met a

moose.

"Moose," he said, "you are just what I need for my mice."

Little  m saw a

merry-go-round.

"Let's ride on the merry-go-round," he said.

He found some money.

And they all went for a ride on
the merry-go-round.

Then Little m looked up
and saw the moon.

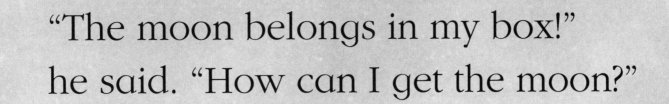

"The moon belongs in my box!"
he said. "How can I get the moon?"

Just then,

Little **m** met a magician.

"The moon is too big
for your box," said the magician.

"But I will take you to the moon in my

magic moon machine."

And he did!

He took them all the way to the moon.

Some magic!

monkey

mouse

moose

moon

magician

mouse

magic moon machine

mouse

monkey

mouse

monkey

Can you read these words with Little 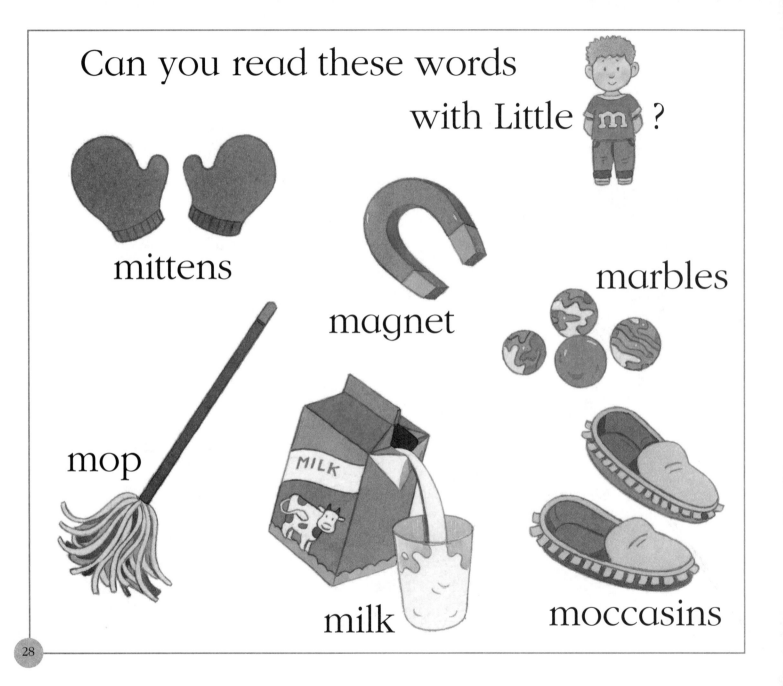 ?

mittens

magnet

marbles

mop

milk

moccasins

marshmallow

macaroni

mug

microscope

motorcycle

mustard

mat

magazine

Aa Bb Cc Dd Ee Ff

Nn Oo Pp Qq Rr Ss Tt

ABC My First Steps to READING®